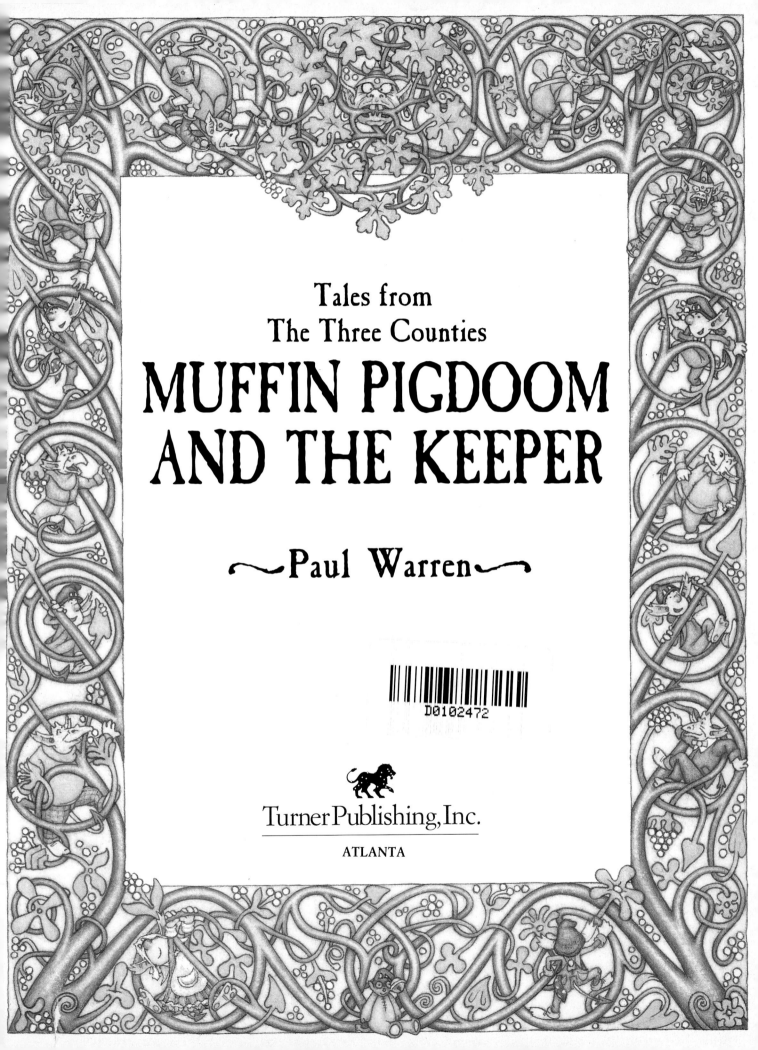

Tales from
The Three Counties

MUFFIN PIGDOOM
AND THE KEEPER

~Paul Warren~

Turner Publishing, Inc.

ATLANTA

Muffin Pigdoom was up at daybreak.

"Come on," he called as he tumbled out of bed and ran around the house. "It's a lovely morning!"

"Go away," grumbled his sister, Camilla.

"It's too early," Muffin's brother, Festus, complained.
Muffin's parents pulled the covers closer, but his Uncle
Carbuncle stretched and got up.

"All right, Muffin," he said sleepily. "Breakfast time."

After breakfast the spring cleaning began. Muffin was keen to join in, but sometimes he got in the way.

"Let me help," he said, standing on his father's tail.

Just then there was a loud knocking at the front door. Uncle Carbuncle looked anxious.

"That sounds like the Urgs," he said.

The front door flew open and in burst the Urgs. They caused a frightful commotion until one ugly brute, bigger than the rest, stepped forward.

"Silence!" he shouted. "I'm Captain Scumble. I'm here to collect your Spring Tax. Pay up or you'll go to the Assizes!"

Muffin turned pale. He'd heard that people who went to the Assizes were sent away for years.

His father protested angrily, "We can't afford your Spring Tax. This purse contains all we have in the world."

Captain Scumble
snatched the purse away.
"This will do nicely,"
he growled. "Fetch the Keeper!"
At that a wild-looking fellow with a sack emerged from
the crowd and sang in a harsh, croaking voice:

Studs the Goblin picks his nose,
With his bag he comes and goes;
He's not worried if you're sad—
But lack of gold makes him mad!

With long bony fingers the Keeper grabbed the purse
and thrust it into his sack.

"Let that be a lesson to you," Captain Scumble said
sternly, and with that he turned and led his troop
out of the house and up the road
to Ratley Bagford.

Although Muffin was frightened, the sight of the Keeper's sack also made him very cross. Those Urgs were so nasty, so greedy. Before his parents could stop him, he slipped out of the door and ran after them.

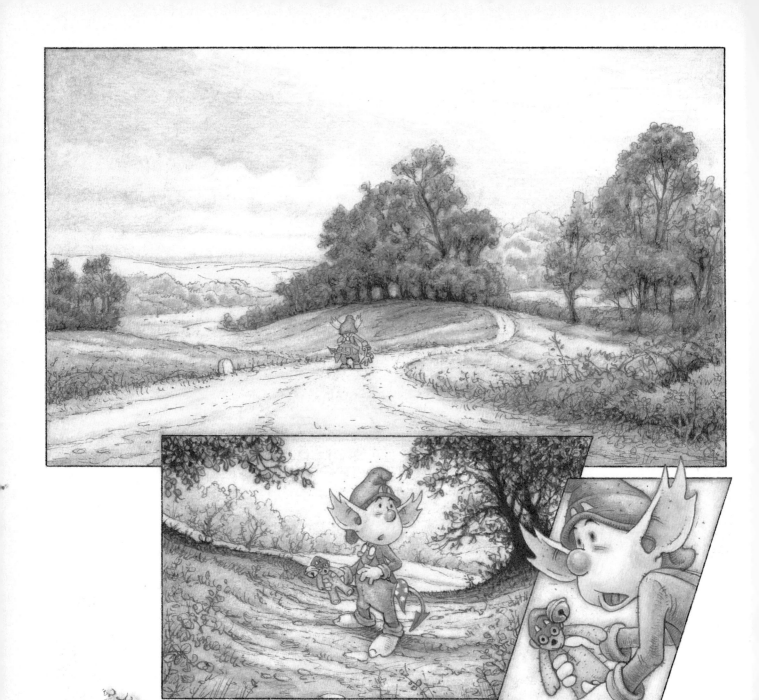

The Urgs traveled quickly on their long bent legs, and soon Muffin was left far behind. He paused to catch his breath.

"Hello, Muffin."

"Pustule! What are you doing?"

His friend peeped out from behind the bushes.

"Hiding!" he whispered. "Urgs went by, lots of them."

"One went over the heath toward Hobbs End—a nasty-looking creature with a sack!"

"The Keeper!" cried Muffin. "That's the one I'm after."

Muffin ran and ran, and soon he found himself on the edge of Darkling Wood. This was a scary place, and his mother had warned him about it many times, but today he ran on without stopping.

He had not gone far when he heard strange sounds
close by. Stepping carefully, he crept up to a large tree
and peered around the trunk.

He opened his eyes wide.

There was the Keeper, down on all fours, scratching at a hole in the ground.

He unearthed a small box, and his yellow eyes rolled with delight. "Gold!" he cackled as he emptied the box into his sack.

Muffin watched closely, for among the shining coins he could see his father's purse. "He's robbed *lots* of people!" thought Muffin.

At last the Keeper got up. He threw the sack
over his shoulder and with a terrible laugh strode into the woods.
The trees pressed in closely as Muffin struggled after him.
Tangled roots and branches plucked at Muffin's arms and legs,
and it was hard going. "I wonder where I am," he thought.
Suddenly the Keeper stopped. "What is it?" Muffin wondered.

Muffin hid behind a bush and his heart skipped a beat,
for ahead was a clearing, and in the clearing was a warty
old thunder-lizard as big as a house.

Muffin had never seen such a thing before,
and he wondered what it usually ate for breakfast.
Luckily, the thunder-lizard was fast asleep.

Suddenly a voice hissed, "Don't move!" Then two friendly faces peered cautiously from the leaves.

"Fergus and Fungus!" said Muffin. "What are you doing?"

"We didn't mean to startle you," whispered Fergus. "But we've just seen an Urg go by."

"That's the Keeper," said Muffin grimly. "He's stolen my Dad's purse. I'm following him to get it back."

"We need a plan to catch that Urg," said Fergus.

"There's a dead-end tunnel with an iron gate at the Old Mine," said Fungus. "It's perfect for a trap!"

"How do we get him there?" Muffin asked doubtfully.

"What if I make noises like a wounded animal?" said Fergus. "He's sure to follow. He won't miss the chance of a free meal."

"That's it!" cried Muffin. "Come on!"

"But walk quietly past the thunder-lizard," said Fungus. "I'd hate to be the one who wakes *him* up."

They tiptoed through the clearing
and heard the Keeper grunting and puffing ahead.

"He's slowing down," said Fergus. "Now's our chance."

He ran ahead, and Muffin and Fungus crept quietly from the
path. Now the trees began to thin, and soon they emerged
to see the mouth of a cave yawning in a rocky hillside.

"Be careful," warned Fungus. "There are lots of deep holes around here. If you fall in one, you'll be lost forever."

Muffin pricked up his ears. He could hear noises in the forest now: howling and the sound of a sack being shaken.

Fungus hissed, "Run for the gate and look for a stone. When the Urg's inside we'll jam it shut!"

Muffin and Fungus separated, and a moment later Fergus burst from the trees and raced toward the cave. Behind him came the Keeper—*crash!*—charging up the hill.

"What have we here?" he said in a hideous voice as he stepped into the cave. "Something for the pot?"

Immediately Fungus sprang up. "Quick, Fergus! Run!
He's in the trap! Push! *Heave!*"

But the gate would not budge. It was old, and the hinges
were rusty.

"A fine trap this is," laughed the Keeper, grabbing hold
of the twins. "All you've caught is yourselves!"

From his hiding place, Muffin watched, aghast. What could he do to save his friends?

Quickly, he turned and ran to the clearing where the thunder-lizard was sleeping.

"Wake up! Wake up!" he shouted.

The monster grunted and raised its head. "Can't catch me!" shouted Muffin. He crossed his eyes and stuck out his tongue. "I hope this trick works," he thought, then ran for dear life.

Meanwhile, the Keeper was dangling Fergus and
Fungus over the edge of a deep hole.

"You'll rue the day you tangled with me," he taunted.

Suddenly he heard shouts and saw Muffin running
from the woods straight toward him.

"Bless my boots," he laughed. "If it isn't another one."

But his smile soon vanished when he saw the thunder-
lizard crashing through the trees behind Muffin.

Filled with panic, he dropped the twins on the ground
and dived into the hole. Fergus and Fungus ran with
Muffin into the cave to hide.

Finding no bones to crunch, the thunder-lizard crashed
angrily back into the woods.

They waited until everything was quiet and then nervously emerged from the cave.

"Look there," hissed Muffin, pointing to the hole. "Can you see what I see?"

Down below, the Keeper clung desperately to a root.

"Give me a hand," he shouted.

"I want my Dad's money back first," said Muffin.

The Keeper's yellow eyes flashed. "Take it," he said.

Muffin reached into the hole. He untied the neck of the sack and withdrew his father's purse.

"Now give me a hand," demanded the Keeper.

"I can't help you *and* that great sack," said Muffin. "You'll have to pass it up first."

"Never," growled the Keeper, and he shook with rage. "It's mine, all mine!"

"Quickly," said Muffin. "That root won't hold forever."

But the Keeper didn't answer. The root creaked, there was a loud *crack!* and he was gone.

"Silly creature," said Muffin. "But at least
he didn't get this." He shook the purse triumphantly
and smiled and thanked his friends. Fergus and Fungus
went with Muffin to the crossroads at Deep Ditchford.
To avoid the woods, he took the long way back.

It was dusk when Muffin came racing over the heath
to Pigdoom Cottage and home.

"We thought you were gone for good!" cried Mrs. Pigdoom
as he ran into her arms.

Muffin smiled and showed them his father's purse.

"I've had such an adventure!" he told them.

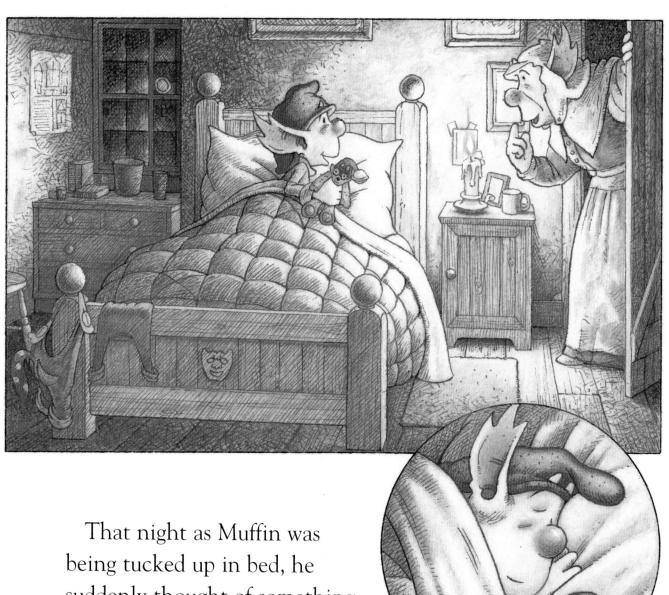

That night as Muffin was
being tucked up in bed, he
suddenly thought of something.

"Mom," he asked, "who is
Studs the Goblin?"

Mrs. Pigdoom had forgotten
the Keeper's strange song.

"A friend of Captain Scumble's, I shouldn't wonder."

She chuckled and kissed him on the nose. "Whatever will
you think of next?"

THE THRE

BADLAND GAP

THE
BLUFFS

THE DISTANT HILLS

Toad-in-the-Hole

Lo

Little
Doubting

Brimstone

Pig's Eye

Ratley

Ratley Bagford

Scrotty Codfield

Warty Orton

Festerbridge

Brackenbridge

Hogs Bottom

URGTOP

Ditchwater

GREENMERE

Midmarsh

Deep Ditch